A Moment in Time

Written by Jennifer Butenas

Illustrated by Charlotte Cheng

Once upon a time
There was a family of four
Rockin' on their rockers
Outside their front door.

The porch floor creaked,
The rockers swayed

Beneath a glorious sky—
'Twas a dazzling day!

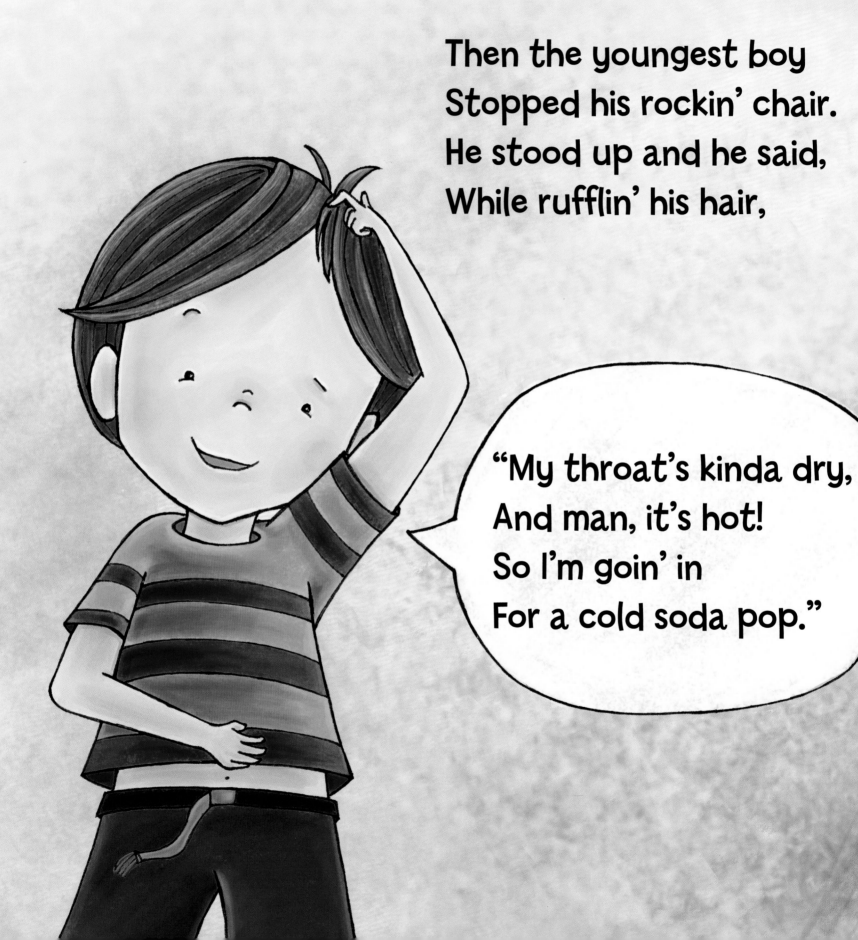

He leaped and he hooted.
He marched high and bold,
Lookin' for a can of
Soda freezin' cold!

He walked into the house
With a flip and a flop,
Grabbed a can from the fridge,
And left with a hop.

Back to his rocker
He made a beeline,
Sippin' on his sugar
And feelin' so fine.

He wiped all the sticky
From his mouth with his hand,
And he rocked as if listenin'
To a slow, easy band.

It was a *sugary-boogery,*
Thirst-quenchin'
Moment in time.

With a huge blast of might
And a mischievous glance,

He jumped
off the porch . . .

And he started to ... *dance!*

He hipped to the right
And he shook to the left.
Those cool dance moves
Were his best ones yet!

As bright as sunshine,
Smile wide as the sea,
This boy had rhythm
And immense *en-er-gy!*

With a twirl and a swirl,
Lookin' up to the sky,
He danced with style,
Thrusting fists up high!

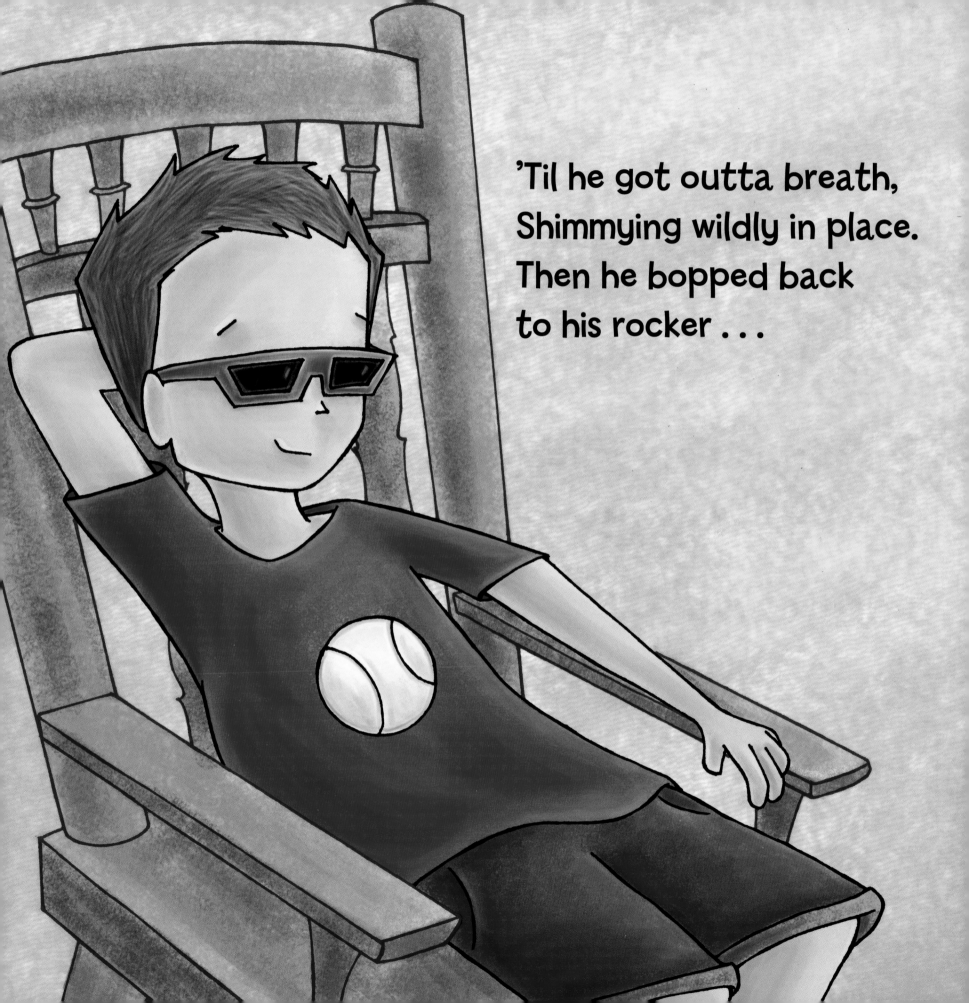

'Til he got outta breath,
Shimmying wildly in place.
Then he bopped back
to his rocker . . .

... At a slow, easy pace.

With his head tilted back
And his shades in place,
This boy was cool—
A fine lookin' ace!

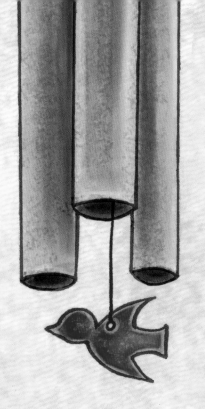

It was a shockin' and a rockin',
Silly-minilie
Moment in time.

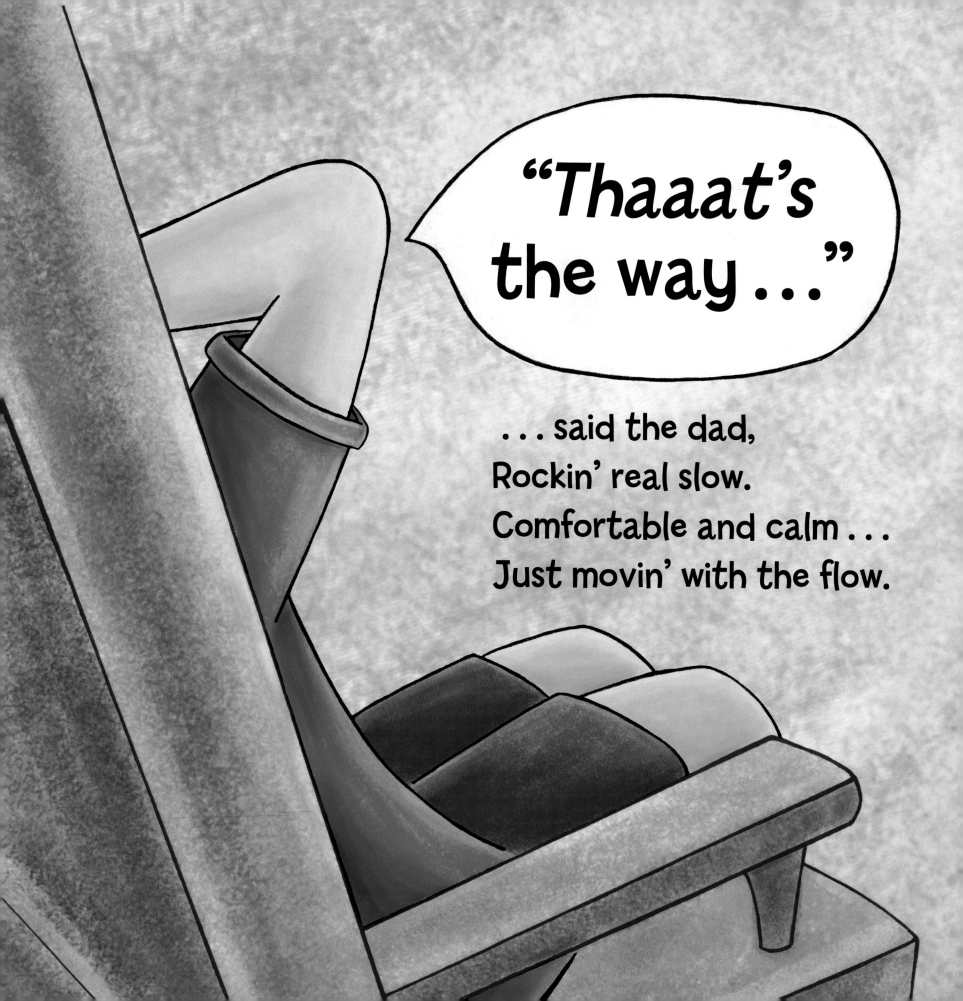

The warm sun shone
On his calm, cool face.
He was quiet and peaceful
As he **stopped** in place . . .

His brow was smooth
As he listened to the breeze.
He was *sooooo* relaxed
That he couldn't even sneeze.

His eyes were closed
And his breathing slow.
His muscles were restin'
From his head to his toe.

It was a lazy-manazy,
snorin' mornin'
Moment in time.

"What a great picture!"

. . . Said the mom with glee.
She stood up with her camera,
Putting down her iced tea.

She glided off the porch
And looked back at her clan.

The youngest thinkin', "Soda,"

The other rockin' to his band.

Dad was asleep,
Snoring heavy and fine.

We're Expecting!

and caught . . .

a moment in time!

For my children, Zac, Ben and Emilee.
—Jennifer

For my parents, and their unconditional love.
—Charlotte

Written by Jennifer Butenas
Illustrated by Charlotte Cheng
Book design by Jill Ronsley, suneditwrite.com

ISBN: 978-0-9840039-0-7
Library of Congress Control Number: 2011916211

First Edition 2012
Printed and bound in the USA

Published by The Perfect Moment, LLC
www.ThePerfectMomentllc.com
29 Portsmouth Ave Suite 177
Stratham New Hampshire 03885

The Perfect Moment, LLC